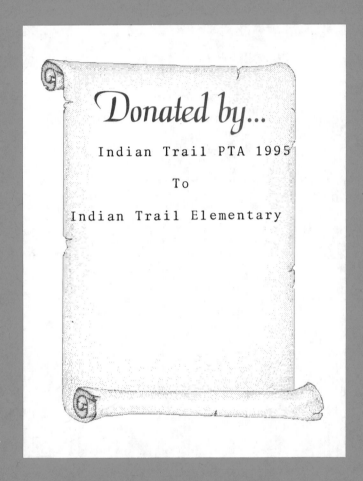

Donated by...

Indian Trail PTA 1995

To

Indian Trail Elementary

TAILYPO!

Retold by Jan Wahl • Illustrated by Wil Clay

HENRY HOLT AND COMPANY • NEW YORK

For Ruth Williams
with lots of love
—J. W.

Lovingly dedicated
to my children—
Michael, Tina, Alecia,
Melinda, Tamorah and Donato
—W. C.

Text copyright © 1991 by Jan Wahl
Illustrations copyright © 1991 by Wil Clay
All rights reserved, including the right to reproduce
this book or portions thereof in any form.

Published by Henry Holt and Company, Inc.,
115 West 18th Street, New York, New York 10011.
Published in Canada by Fitzhenry & Whiteside Limited,
195 Allstate Parkway, Markham, Ontario L3R 4T8.

Library of Congress Cataloging-in-Publication Data
Wahl, Jan.
    Tailypo! / retold by Jan Wahl; illustrated by Wil Clay.
    Summary: A strange varmint haunts the woodsman who
lopped off its tail.
    ISBN 0-8050-0687-7
    [1. Folklore—United States.]   I. Clay, Wil, ill.   II. Title.
PZ8.1.W126   Tai   1991
398.21′0973—dc 20   90-39491

Henry Holt books are available at special discounts
for bulk purchases for sales promotions, premiums,
fund-raising, or educational use. Special editions
or book excerpts can also be created to specification.

Printed in the United States of America
on acid-free paper. ∞

10 9 8 7 6 5 4 3

ONCE way down in
the big woods of Tennessee
lived an old man all by himself
in a cabin with one room

and that was his parlor,
his sitting room,
his bedroom, his dining room,
and his kitchen, too.
At the end of the room
was a high, deep, open fireplace
and that's where he cooked
and ate his supper—

and one night
after he ate his supper
there crept through the cracks
in the logs a Creature

with a *great, big, long* tail.

When he saw that Creature,
the old man grabbed his hatchet
and WHUMP!
With one lick he cut that
thing's tail off!

Quick as wind he threw
salt and pepper over that tail
and cooked it and ate it up.

He didn't sleep very long
'fore he heard something crawling
up the side of his cabin—
scritch scritch scritch.

He heard it say,
*"Tailypo, tailypo.
All I want is
my tailypo."*

He had three dogs—
Uno, Ino, and Sis Comptico Calico.
"Huh! Huh!" he called the dogs
and they jumped off the floor
and chased that Creature
over to the woods.
Well, the old man went back to sleep.

In the middle of the night
he woke hearing something
right above his cabin door,
trying to get in.
He heard it *scritch scritch
scritch*, and moan,
*"Tailypo! Tailypo!
All I want is my tailypo!"*

Again he called his dogs: "Huh! *Huh!*"
They came busting round the corner
of the house and went tearing down
the gate after that THING!

They chased it over to the swamp
and the old man went back to bed.

Along about morning he woke up
hearing SOMETHING down in the
big swamp, saying,
"You know! I know!
All I want is my tailypo!"

Again that old man called his dogs: "Huh! *Huh!*"

But this time they didn't come
because that thing grabbed them!
And the old man went back to sleep.

Hey! Just before daylight he woke up hearing *something* right there in his room, climbing up the bed covers, going SCRITCH SCRITCH SCRITCH.

And he looked over the foot
of the bed and saw
two little pointed ears,
and in a minute
two big, round, fiery eyes.

He tried to call his dogs
but was too scared to holler.

That thing kept creeping up
till by and by it was
'most on top of that old man!

And then it said in a low, low voice,
"Tailypo, tailypo.
All I want is my tailypo."

Well! That old man
sat up hollering,
"I DON'T HAVE YOUR TAILYPO!"

And that thing said,
"Yes, you have,"
and it jumped on that old man
and gobbled him up.

And some folks say
it got back its tailypo.